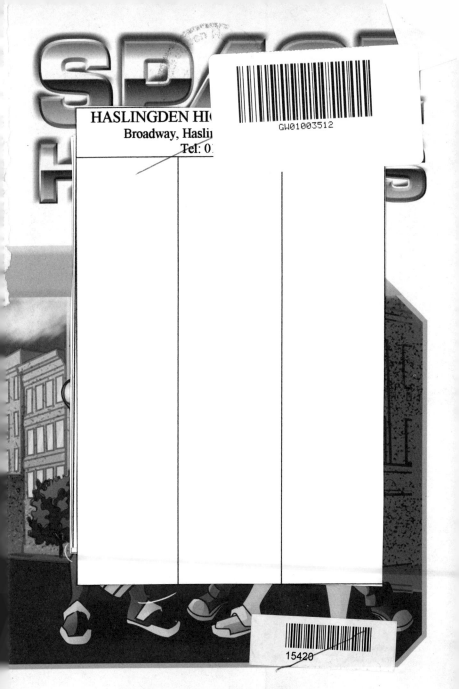

HASLINGDEN HI
Broadway, Hasli
Tel: 0

TOMMY DONBAVAND

Helping Everyone Achieve ● ■ ■

NASEN House, 4/5 Amber Business Village, Amber Close, Amington,
Tamworth, Staffordshire, B77 4RP

Rising Stars UK Ltd.
7 Hatchers Mews, Bermondsey Street, London SE1 3GS
www.risingstars-uk.com

Published 2014

Author: Tommy Donbavand
Cover design: Sarah Garbett @ Sg Creative Services
Illustrations: Alan Brown for Advocate Art
Text design and typesetting: Sarah Garbett @ Sg Creative Services
Publisher: Fiona Lazenby
Editorial consultants: Jane Friswell and Dee Reid
Editorial: Fiona Tomlinson and Sarah Chappelow

British Library Cataloguing in Publication Data.
A CIP record of this book is available from the British Library.

ISBN: 978-1-78339-327-5

Printed in the UK by Ashford Colour Press Ltd, Gosport, Hampshire

CONTENTS

MEET THE SPACE HOPPERS

DAN

Name: Dan Fireball
Rank: Captain
Age: 12
Home planet: Earth
Most likely to: hide behind the Captain's chair and ask timidly, "Are we there yet?"

ASTRA

Name: Astra Moon
Rank: Second Officer
Age: 11
Home planet: The Moon
Most likely to: face up to The Geezer, strike a karate pose and say, "Bring it on!"

HS INFINITY

WANTED

THE GEEZER

VOLT

Name: Volt
Rank: Agent
Age: Really old!
Home planet: Venus
Most likely to: puff steam from his shoulder exhausts and announce, "Hop completed!"

GUS

Name: Gus Buster
Rank: Head of COSMIC
Age: 15
Home planet: Earth
Most likely to: suddenly appear on the view screen and yell, "Fireball, where are you?"

Greetings new recruits!

My name is Volt and I shall be your cyber-teacher for today.

You should read this section because if you wish to become COSMIC agents you must know the history of the Solar System.

VOLT

Long ago, adults used to be in charge of everything. They had jobs, ran governments and were in charge of television remote controls.

Children were forced to stay in school until the age of 18. They had to do everything their parents told them. They were only given small amounts of currency, known as "pocket money".

There were lots of problems. Adults polluted the Earth and then went on to do the same – or even worse – on the remaining eight planets of our Solar System. In fact, for a long time, adults even refused to call Pluto a real planet!

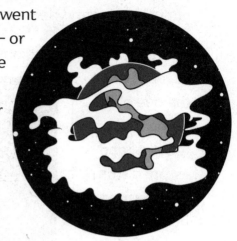

So, in the year 2281, the children took over.

Adults were made to retire at the age of 18 and were sent to retirement homes on satellites in space. Children just needed three years at school, so most children were working by the time they were eight years old.

The Solar System quickly became a much happier, safer and cleaner place to live.

However, not all of the adults liked having to retire at the age of 18. Some of them rebelled and escaped from their retirement homes on satellites in space.  They began to cause trouble and commit crimes.

That's why **COSMIC** was created:

Crimes

    Of

        Serious

           Magnitude

             Investigation

               Company

The worst of these villains was known as The Geezer. The purpose of COSMIC was to stop The Geezer from committing crimes.

Members of COSMIC flew around the Solar System solving mysteries and bringing badly behaved adults to justice. The COSMIC spaceships could navigate an invisible series of magnetic tunnels called the Hop Field, so they were called Space Hoppers.

I myself, was a member of one such team of Space Hoppers, alongside the famous agents - Dan Fireball and Astra Moon.

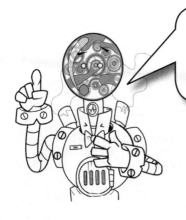

If you turn the page, you can read about a mission that delivered us nothing but trouble ...

CHAPTER 1

FUNNY STUFF

HS INFINITY DATA LOG

MISSION REPORT 6:

PANIC ON PLUTO

REPORT BEGINS ...

Astra Moon stepped on to the command deck of the HS Infinity, loaded down with computer keyboards. She dumped them on to her desk, then began to connect them to her terminal, one at a time.

"I don't suppose you know anything about my sudden computer malfunction, Dan?" she said.

From his chair near the front of the deck, Captain Dan Fireball said nothing.

"I bet you messed with my computer," Astra told the Captain crossly.

An old brass robot crossed over to Astra, balanced on a single wheel. Clouds of steam erupted from twin exhaust pipes at his shoulders. "May I be of assistance, Miss Astra?" he enquired.

Astra heard a giggle. She gave the Captain an angry look.

"That depends," said Astra, trying the third keyboard in her pile. "You wouldn't happen to know why I'm having trouble writing my weekly report, would you?"

"I don't understand Miss Astra," said Volt. "What kind of trouble are you having?"

"The kind of trouble where, every time I try to type up details of our last mission, all that appears on my screen is this…"

11

She spun her computer terminal round for Volt to see. The robot flicked a pair of half-moon shaped spectacles up in front of his sparking electric eye globes and began to read.

Astra's computer screen said:

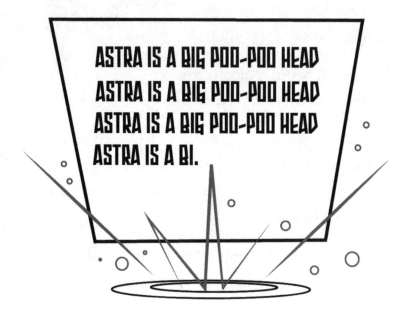

ASTRA IS A BIG POO-POO HEAD
ASTRA IS A BIG POO-POO HEAD
ASTRA IS A BIG POO-POO HEAD
ASTRA IS A BI.

"And you're certain that is not what you intended to type?" asked Volt.

This time, the Captain laughed out loud.

"But I know exactly who is responsible," Astra called out. "He must have switched my keyboard for a trick version."

The tiny speaker on Astra's communication bracelet crackled into life. "Can you get me a piece of cake, please?"

Astra frowned at the bracelet. "Is that you, Dan?" she asked, "Why are you using your bracelet?"

"Sore throat," came the reply through the bracelet speaker. "Now, about that cake ..."

"I'm working!" cried Astra. "Or, at least, I'm trying to. If you think I'm going all the way down to the kitchen to fetch you a piece of cake, you're dafter than I thought."

"But I want cake!" demanded Dan.

"Then get it yourself!" snapped Astra.

"Excuse me, Second Officer," said the voice through the bracelet. "Who is the Captain of this ship?"

Astra's cheeks flushed red. "I'll get you back for this, Dan Fireball!" She jumped up and stomped to the exit doors. They whooshed open to reveal ...

... Captain Dan Fireball, wearing a t-shirt and shorts and talking into a communication bracelet. "A nice big piece of cream cake, please!" he giggled.

"What?" cried Astra. "How did you ...?" She looked back across the deck where she could see the figure of the Captain, relaxing in his chair. "Then who's that?"

The chair spun round, and a boy aged around nine jumped up. He had fair hair, just like Dan's, and he was wearing an oversized COSMIC Captain's uniform.

"Who's that?" demanded Astra.

"Meet my little brother, Felix," beamed Dan, hurrying over. "I'm taking him bowling after we've finished work today."

"And having some fun at my expense first," said Astra crossly.

"Yeah, sorry that was me!" said Felix, producing a computer keyboard from beneath the captain's chair. "This is yours; it'll type properly for you."

"Thanks," said Astra, reaching out to take the keyboard. Felix's entire hand came with it.

Astra screamed and dropped the keyboard and hand.

"You were right, Dan!" grinned Felix, as he slid his real hand out of the sleeve of the captain's uniform. "You said she'd fall for it."

"The old fake hand trick!" laughed Dan, snatching up the rubber hand and wiggling it in Astra's face. "It's a comedy classic."

"Yeah," grumbled Astra, picking up her keyboard and heading back to her desk. She deleted the rude text from her screen, and began to write her report.

The sound of laughter made her look up. Dan and Felix were now trying to force the rubber hand over the end of one of Volt's metal arms.

"Two of them," she muttered. "That's all I need!"

CHAPTER 2

DELIVERANCE

Suddenly, the vast view screen at the front of the command deck burst into life, and a large, serious face appeared. It was Chief Gus Buster, the head of COSMIC.

Dan quickly pushed Felix down behind the captain's chair. "Hide!" he hissed.

"Chief!" said Astra. "What's up?"

"There's a problem on ..." began The Chief, then he stopped and stared at Dan. "Why are you out of uniform, Captain Fireball?"

Dan glanced down at his t-shirt and shorts. Felix was still wearing his official COSMIC uniform.

"I'm ... er ... practising working undercover, Chief." said Dan.

"That's right, Chief," said Astra. "Any time you need an undercover idiot for a mission, Dan is ready to go."

"Idiot or not, I need you back in uniform, Captain Fireball," snapped the Chief. "Someone is delivering pizzas to Pluto."

Dan blinked. "And you need us there to help eat them?"

"Don't be ridiculous!" the Chief barked. "It's not just pizzas being delivered - there are books, flowers, washing machines, cars, building materials and more. Container after container of goods that the people who live on Pluto haven't ordered."

"Sounds like someone's playing a prank," suggested Astra.

"Exactly," said the Chief. "But this prank could have very serious consequences. Pluto is approaching terminal mass ..."

"Terminal mass?" said Dan, looking blank. "And that's bad is it?"

Volt wheeled up to the view screen. "It is indeed, Master Dan," he said, tapping a series of commands into the keyboard in the wall.

The image on the screen changed to show the planet Pluto: small, purple, and floating alone in the outer limits of the Solar System.

20

"As you will be aware, when adults were in charge of the Solar System they decided that Pluto was too small to be considered a planet."

"Really?" said Dan. "Then what did they call it?"

"They called Pluto a dwarf planet, Master Dan," Volt explained.

The image zoomed in to one of Pluto's major towns. Crowds of short, lilac-skinned Plutonions demonstrated angrily about the decision, carrying banners with slogans like:

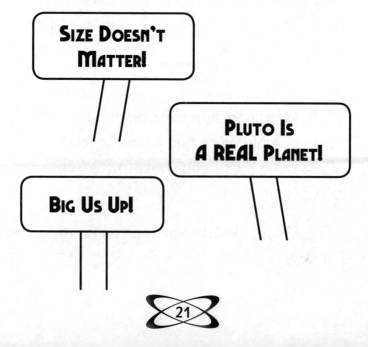

SIZE DOESN'T MATTER!

PLUTO IS A REAL PLANET!

BIG US UP!

"As you can see, the population of Pluto were not happy about their home not being a real planet," Volt told them. "The people began building to try to increase the overall size of Pluto, and become a planet again."

Tall skyscrapers appeared on the screen. Every available space had been built on, transforming the already busy towns into huge, bustling cities.

"That looks like London, back on Earth," said Dan.

"Or New York," said Astra.

"Exactly, Master Dan," said Volt. "The problem is that cities of such a size are simply too big for Pluto. As the mass of the planet grew, it came dangerously close to tipping out of its usual orbit and floating off into space."

The Chief's face returned to the screen. "Which is why Pluto now has a strict goods in and goods out policy," he said. "The planet cannot risk growing any further."

Dan grew pale. "Terminal mass!" he gasped, finally understanding. "When Pluto gets so heavy that it falls out of its orbit."

"And now someone has started delivering tonnes of new stuff there," said Astra.

"Any idea who's doing it?" asked Dan.

"We're working on it," said the Chief. "We scanned the outer Solar System and discovered a group of ten ships, hovering just outside of normal detection range."

Gus Buster tapped on his own keyboard, and brought a blurred, black and white image up on the screen. It showed dozens of white blobs hovering a few light years' away from Pluto's surface.

Dan squinted. "Who are they?" he asked. "An invasion fleet?"

"It's impossible to tell," said Astra.

"I may be able to assist, Miss Astra," said Volt, producing a pair of magnifying glasses. He peered at the image through them. "Oh dear ..."

"What is it?" asked Dan.

"I think you should take a look at this, sir," said Volt.

Dan and Astra looked at the image on the screen through the robot's brass-rimmed glasses. The picture instantly looked both clearer and closer - revealing that each of the ships was a rocket-powered retirement home.

One of the retirement homes sat in front of the others. Astra looked hard, and could just make out a sign hammered into the lawn behind the white wooden fence.

"Shady Acres," she read aloud.

Captain Dan Fireball took a deep breath. "The Geezer!" he groaned.

CHAPTER 3

IN THE BALANCE

"**B**etter get your uniform on, Dan," said Astra, hurrying back to her desk. "We'll be Hopping to Pluto in just under two minutes." She began to calculate the Hop co-ordinates on her computer.

Felix appeared from behind the captain's chair, looking alarmed.

"But, what about Felix?" said Dan.

"He'll have to put his own clothes back on," said Astra.

"No, I mean what do we do with him?" said Dan.

"Well, he can't come with us," said Astra. "He's not Hop trained."

"And I can't just leave him behind," said Dan. "There's no one to look after him."

"He's nine years old!" said Astra. "Doesn't he have a job?"

"I work for a computer security company," said Felix, taking off the captain's uniform.

"That's why he's so good at hacking into things, like your keyboard," said Dan.

"Then can't he go back to work?" asked Astra.

"It's my day off," said Felix. "Dan's taking me bowling."

Astra went back to her calculations. "I don't think you'll be going bowling today."

Felix turned to Dan. "Really?"

Dan climbed into his red COSMIC jumpsuit. "It doesn't look like it," he said. "Space Hopper duties have to come first."

"And Felix isn't a Space Hopper," Astra pointed out. "He can't come to Pluto with us."

Volt wheeled across the command deck. "Actually, Miss Astra, there is a way that Master Felix could travel with us. The COSMIC rules allow the Captain to make any member of the public a crew member for a short period of time."

Dan looked surprised. "So, if I recruited Felix, he could stay with us today?"

"That is correct, Master Dan." said Volt.

"Brilliant!" exclaimed Dan. "Then I make Felix the Deputy Captain,"

"Whoa," said Astra. "Wait a minute …"

"Is that it?" asked Felix. "Am I Deputy Captain of the Infinity?"

"For the moment, yes," said Volt.

"Hang on …" said Astra.

Felix spun to face her. "Which means I'm your boss!" he said gleefully. "Now, about that piece of cake ..."

"No eating during spaceflight!" growled Astra. "Prepare to Hop!"

She slammed her palm down on a large yellow button on her desk. The HS Infinity leapt sideways into one of the invisible magnetic tunnels that make up the Hop Field, connecting every planet and moon in the Solar System. Within seconds, the ship was whizzing along.

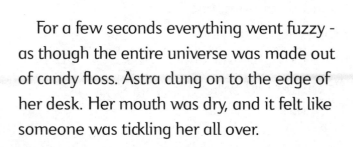

For a few seconds everything went fuzzy - as though the entire universe was made out of candy floss. Astra clung on to the edge of her desk. Her mouth was dry, and it felt like someone was tickling her all over.

Dan and Felix gripped the arms of the captain's chair tightly. Everything swayed from left to right then an image of Pluto flickered into place on the view screen.

"We have arrived at Pluto," announced Volt as the Captain and his new Deputy sank to the floor.

Astra approached the view screen. "Look at that!" she gasped.

Dan pulled himself upright and stared. "That's not ..."

"What?" asked Felix, standing up and trying to control his shaking legs.

On the screen, Pluto was surrounded by hundreds of unmanned delivery drones, each carrying more items to overload the tiny planet and send it spinning off course.

Space crafts of all shapes and sizes were taking off from cities across the planet, as Plutonions hastily removed the unwanted deliveries and dumped them on to one of Pluto's five tiny moons.

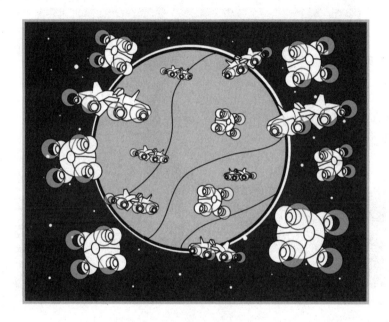

"They can't keep doing that for much longer," said Astra. "The moons will collapse inwards under the weight."

Suddenly, the speakers burst into life and a low, creaking sound filled the command deck. As the crew watched, the planet below began to tilt slowly to one side.

"It's started!" cried Astra. "Pluto is falling out of its orbit."

"We have to stop any more deliveries getting in!" said Dan. "Astra, can you pilot us in closer to the surface?"

"Of course," said Astra. "But why?"

"If we can get in the way of those drones, we can stop them delivering their goods," explained Dan.

"Crossing the flight path of another space vehicle is an extremely risky thing to do," said Astra. "But, in this case, I can't think of anything else. Strap in, boys!"

CHAPTER 4

STRIKE

Dan and Felix raced for the captain's chair as Astra switched HS Infinity out of automatic pilot mode. She gripped the large joystick and thrust the controls away from herself.

The HS Infinity shot forward, hurtling towards the swarm of delivery ships. Dan pushed Felix to one side and jumped into his chair, locking the seatbelt across himself.

"What about me?" cried Felix.

Dan pulled his younger brother on to his lap and wrapped his arms tightly around him.

The HS Infinity began to rattle as it bumped across the space lanes, racing for its target position. The low creaking sound became a deep groan as Pluto tilted even further.

Suddenly, the screen hissed and the view of the planet was replaced by the face of an adult. An adult wearing a grey cardigan. Dan couldn't see the man's feet, but he just knew that the man would be wearing comfy slippers.

"The Geezer!" said Dan.

"Dan Fireball!" barked The Geezer. "You Space Hoppers have caused me enough trouble for ..." He stopped and stared into his camera. "Why have you got a ventriloquist's dummy on your lap?"

"It's not a dummy!" said Dan, pushing Felix off his knee. "It's my brother."

"Oh great!" said The Geezer, rolling his eyes. "Two of them - just what I need!"

"My thoughts exactly!" cried Astra as she battled with the ship's controls. "But the extra Fireball isn't the problem at the moment. You are!"

"Me?" spat The Geezer. "You're the one flying into certain danger. I'm sitting quietly in my retirement home - just as you pesky children told me to."

Astra hit the 'Escape' button on her keyboard. The picture of The Geezer vanished from the view screen, and was replaced with the sight of buzzing delivery drones shooting straight for them.

"Quick!" cried Dan, undoing his seatbelt and jumping up. "Block that one!"

Astra steered the ship to the right, causing the drone to move out of the way, but at once another delivery drone took its place. "Now that one!" shouted Dan, pointing to the top left of the screen.

The HS Infinity jolted to the left sending another drone flying. Instantly, four more drones filled the empty space.

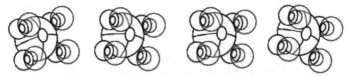

"That one next!" cried Dan, running from one side of the screen to the other. "No, I mean that one ... er ... that one!" He stopped as hundreds of drones began to race past them on all sides.

Behind them, in the distance, sat Shady Acres and the nine other retirement homes. Dan could just imagine the smug grin on The Geezer's face.

"That man called me a dummy!" said Felix, glumly.

"Never mind that!" shouted Astra. "We're in trouble here. There are just too many delivery drones for us to stop."

"He's done it!" Dan sighed, slumping back into his chair. "The Geezer has finally beaten us."

Volt rolled back and forth along the length of the command deck as the HS Infinity lurched left and right. "I'm afraid you are correct, Master Dan," he said as he shot past. "I don't know how we can save Pluto."

"I do!" said Felix. "I'll show that old codger I'm not a dummy." He hurried over to Astra's desk. "Can I use your computer, please?"

"What for?" demanded Astra.

Felix grinned. "I can hack into the system controlling the delivery drones," he said. "I'll order them to return all their goods to the depot."

"Brilliant!" cried Astra, moving out of her seat to allow Felix to sit down. The Deputy Captain began to type furiously at the keyboard. "I hope being a hero makes up for having to miss bowling."

"Felix, are you inside the delivery company's computer system yet?"

"Nearly," said Felix, "I'm just about to recall all the drones."

"Don't!" ordered Dan. "The Geezer and his cronies will just call another company and start ordering stuff all over again. We have to get rid of them."

"That would be ideal," said Astra, "but I don't see how."

"We just have to strike at the boss himself!" beamed Dan. He turned back to his brother. "Command all the drones to deliver their items on the north-west face of the planet - at exactly the same time."

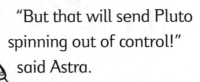
"But that will send Pluto spinning out of control!" said Astra.

"Spinning, yes," winked Dan. "Out of control, no!"

Astra's eyes grew wide as Dan's idea sunk in. "I suppose for once the Fireball brothers might get something right."

She snatched up a microphone and pressed the talk button. "This is the COSMIC Hop Ship, HS Infinity, contacting the population of Pluto on all available channels. Things are about to get a little bumpy, so grab hold of something."

"Okay," said Felix, typing in a final command. "Whenever you're ready."

Dan stepped up to the view screen, closed one eye and peered at the distant retirement homes through the speeding drones. "Deliver!" he commanded.

Felix hit the 'Enter' button, and every drone around Pluto began to dive for the same spot on the planet's surface. As each one landed, it added extra mass to the tiny world, causing it to tumble faster and faster through space - heading straight for the collection of retirement homes. .

"Send a handful of drones a mile to the left," Dan said. "We need a little side spin."

Felix sent the command and Pluto edged slightly to one side as it picked up speed.

The screen hissed and The Geezer's face reappeared. His smug smile had been replaced by a look of pure fear.

"What are you doing, Fireball?" he bellowed.

"Taking my brother bowling!" cried Dan, hitting the 'Escape' key on his own keyboard. The view of Pluto returned just in time to see the planet smash into the retirement homes, sending them hurtling off into deep space.

"Strike!"

exclaimed Dan, Astra and Felix together.

"I'll get you for this, Dan Fireball ..." echoed The Geezer's voice through the speakers as Shady Acres vanished into deep space.

"Okay," said Dan, taking his seat. "Felix, get half of the drones to land on the southeast corner of the planet. Let's gently roll Pluto back into the correct orbit."

"Yes, sir!" said Felix, getting to work.

"Volt," continued Dan, "contact the Chief and tell him we'll be sending the drones and all their deliveries back to the depot once we've put Pluto back in place."

"Right away, Master Dan," said the robot, wheeling back to his own workstation.

"What about me?" asked Astra. "What do you want me to do, Captain?"

Dan thought for a second. "There is one thing ..." he said. "Something Felix said earlier. Something I really think would help right now."

"Sure," said Astra. "Just name it."

A cheeky smile crept across Dan's face, then he tapped a button on his bracelet communicator and spoke into the microphone. "Could you go to the kitchen and get me a nice big piece of cake?"

THE END

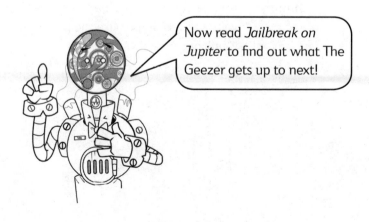

Now read *Jailbreak on Jupiter* to find out what The Geezer gets up to next!

GLOSSARY

consequence — what happens after doing something

demonstrate — gathered in an organised group to protest or complain about something

drone — a machine that is controlled from a distance, by remote control

malfunction — to stop working properly

Plutonian — a creature that lives on the planet Pluto

prank — a practical joke

recruited — asked to work for somebody else

slogan — a short, catchy phrase or motto

terminal mass — the biggest size something can reach before it is destroyed

ventriloquist's dummy — a puppet used by a performer (the ventriloquist) who is able to use their voice to make it look like the puppet is talking

QUIZ QUESTIONS

1   Who has been sitting in the captain's chair?

2   Where is Dan going to take Felix after work?

3   Why did Felix's hand come off?

4   List four items that are being delivered to Pluto.

5   What will happen to Pluto if it reaches terminal mass?

6   Who does Felix work for?

7   What position does Dan recruit Felix into?

8   Where is Felix going to reprogram all of the drones to go?

9   How do the Fireball brothers stop The Geezer?

10   What does Dan ask Astra to do at the end of the story?

ABOUT THE AUTHOR

Tommy Donbavand writes full-time and lives in Lancashire with his family. He is also the author of the 13-book *Scream Street* series (currently in production for TV) and has written numerous books for children and young adults.

For Tommy, the best thing about being an author is getting to spend his days making up adventures for his readers. He also writes for 'The Bash Street Kids' in *The Beano*, which excites him beyond belief!

Find out more about Tommy and his other books at www.tommydonbavand.com

QUIZ ANSWERS

1 Felix, Dan's little brother
2 To go bowling
3 It was a joke, rubber hand.
4 Suggested list: pizza, books, flowers, washing machines, cars, building materials
5 It will fall out of its orbit.
6 A computer security company
7 Deputy Captain
8 The north-west face of the planet
9 They play bowling with Pluto and roll the planet into the retirement home space ships
10 Get him some cake